For the Parsley kids—
Betsy, Jake, Jessie, Carmen, and Owen

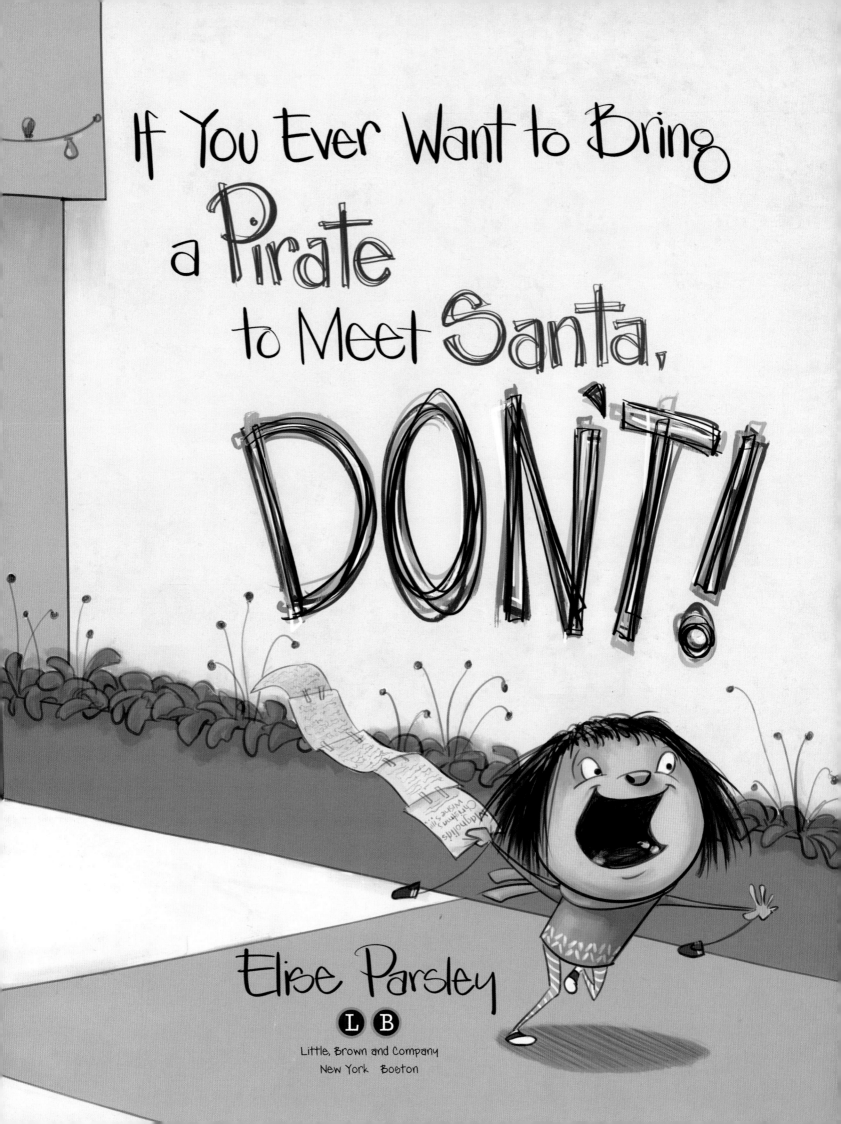

If You Ever Want to Bring a Pirate to Meet Santa, DON'T!

Elise Parsley

LB

Little, Brown and Company
New York   Boston

If your dad says you're going to meet Santa, he means the bearded guy with a red suit and a bag full of treasures.

He does **not** mean *that* guy.
That's a pirate.

If you make friends with a pirate anyway, your dad will tell you that

pirates are on the Naughty List!

You'll tell him it's okay,
and that you will fix that by
the time you meet Santa.
You'll teach this pirate not to pillage
and plunder, or sing loud sea chanties, and
he won't make anybody walk the plank—
cross your heart.

While you wait to meet Santa,
an elf will be handing out candy canes.
You'll say "thank you" and nudge the pirate
to do the same.

He'll say "YARG!"

and
"TOOTH
ROT!"

and finally...

"Thank ye!"

You'll hope he will give those candies back before you meet Santa.

Farther up in line, you'll suggest singing to pass the time.

You'll have to add
"and a merry hog-eye
Christmas to you!"

and hope he will learn Jingle Bells
by the time you meet Santa.

Now the longer you and that pirate wait in line,
the more tired and bored and hungry
you and that pirate will get.

Then
– what ho! –

the pirate will pull
an egg-and-cheese
sandwich from his bag!

You'll remind him that
'tis the season for
giving! He will look
at you...and look
at Santa...

...and then pop that sandwich
right down the hatch.

You will hope you don't starve
before you meet Santa.

Finally,

you will get
to the front
of that line

and meet Santa Claus himself.

Things will be going so well!

Then the elf behind the camera will ask you to smile nicely and say "cheese!"

Then the elf will tell you, no, smile **nicely**, and say "cheeeese!"

He will yell

"just give me one good smile already!"

That's when you'll hear Santa whisper that this is why pirates are on the Naughty List.

And before you know it,

Santa will be walking the plank.

By now, of course, you'll wish you'd have walked right past the bearded guy in a red suit with a bag full of treasure who was really a pirate. By now you'd rather be **stuck in a snowbank** than here with this pirate. And before you can even get the pirate to apologize, Santa and his elves will

March that scallywag
to a chair
and put him
in time-out.

Then do not let him

move from that seat...

until

he changes
his scurvy ways.

After all, pirates **are** on
the Naughty List.